Hug Me

igloobooks

Hug me in the morning,
when soft sunbeams shine.

Hug me by the blossom trees,
when the day is fine.

Hug me when I drop Best Teddy
in a muddy puddle.

Hug me when I've lost my way
and I am in a muddle.

Hug me when my school friends
win all the sports day races.

Hug me when my sister pulls scary monster faces.

Hug me when I fall down,
so you make my tears stop.

Hug me when I've played all day
and I'm too tired to hop.

Hug me on a windy day,
when my friends go flying by.

Hug me
when the golden sun sets
in the evening sky.

Hug me in the evening,
walking on the moonlit path.

Hug me so the bubbles burst
in my bubbly bath.

Hug me when I'm almost ready
to get into bed.

Hug me and whisper softly,
"You're such a sleepyhead."

Hug me as I fall asleep and
I will hug you, too.

There's nothing like a hug to say...

... how much I love you.